No One Knows Where Gobo Goes

By Mark Saltzman · Pictures by Peter Elwell

Muppet Press
Holt, Rinehart and Winston
NEW YORK

For Daniel and Matthew—M.S.

Published by Holt, Rinehart and Winston,
383 Madison Avenue, New York, New York 10017.

Library of Congress Cataloging in Publication Data
Saltzman, Mark.
No one knows where Gobo goes.
Summary: Gobo Fraggle's friends, curious to know
where he goes when he disappears by himself, decide to
follow him one day.
[1. Puppets—Fiction.   2. Solitude—Fiction.
3. Stories in rhyme]   I. Elwell, Peter, ill.
II. Title.
PZ8.3.S175No 1984   [E]   84-6616
ISBN: 0-03-000713-5
First Edition
Printed in the United States of America
1 3 5 7 9 10 8 6 4 2

ISBN 0-03-000713-5

No One Knows
Where Gobo Goes

MY name is Wembley Fraggle,
Fraggle Rock is my address,
And Gobo lives there also.
He's my closest friend, I guess.
He's always there to help me choose
Between a no and yes.

Gobo's an explorer.
He explores things very well.
He usually tells us when
He's leaving for a spell.
But sometimes he just disappears,
To where, he doesn't tell.

So no one knows where Gobo goes
(We Fraggles often say).

Yes, no one knows where Gobo goes
When Gobo goes away.

Now Mokey, Red, and I one day
Were walking underground
When Mokey, in her dreamy way,
Turned to look around.

"Wembley, do you know," she asked,
"Where Gobo might be found?"

Then gloomy Boober wandered up
And said, "Is Gobo here?

I simply cannot understand
How he can disappear.

I hope he's not in trouble deep.
Oh gosh. What's more, oh dear!"

That's typical of Boober.
He comes up with things like that.
If you're enjoying radishes,
He'll say you're getting fat.

You know what sounds like Boober most?

A tuba playing flat.

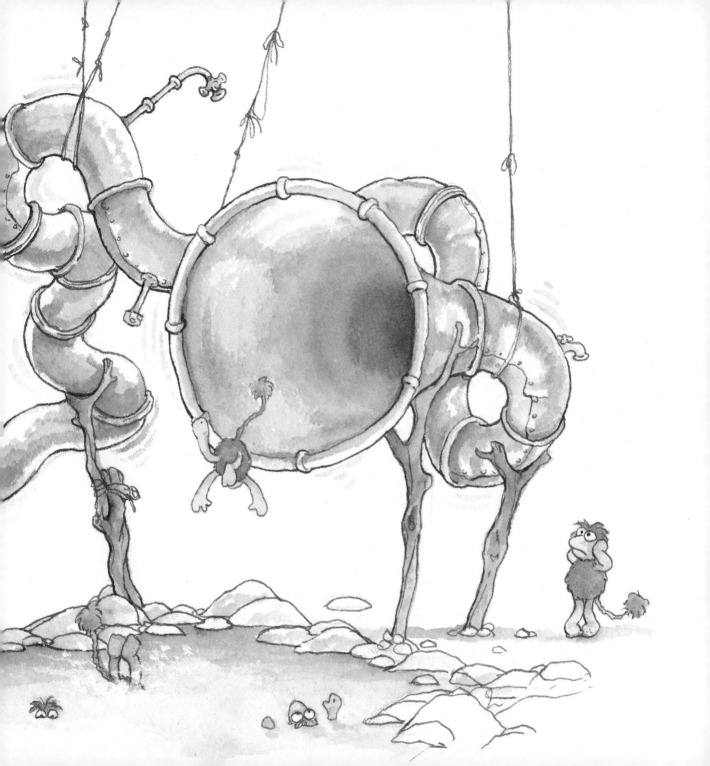

Then Red said, "Yes, where's Gobo?
Wembley! Don't you even care?"
I know that trouble's on the way
Whenever Red is there.

Does Red herself bring trouble on?
Do Fraggle tails have hair?

"I have a thought," Red added.
"Now, here's what I propose.
I think we all should follow him
And learn what no one knows.
So who will dare to come with me
And see where Gobo goes?

"Who will go where Gobo goes

And who will choose to stay?

Who will learn where Gobo goes

When Gobo goes away?"

Well, I was not too pleased with this.
Who wants to be a sneak?
But still, we all were curious,
So later in the week
We noticed Gobo going off
And followed for a peek.

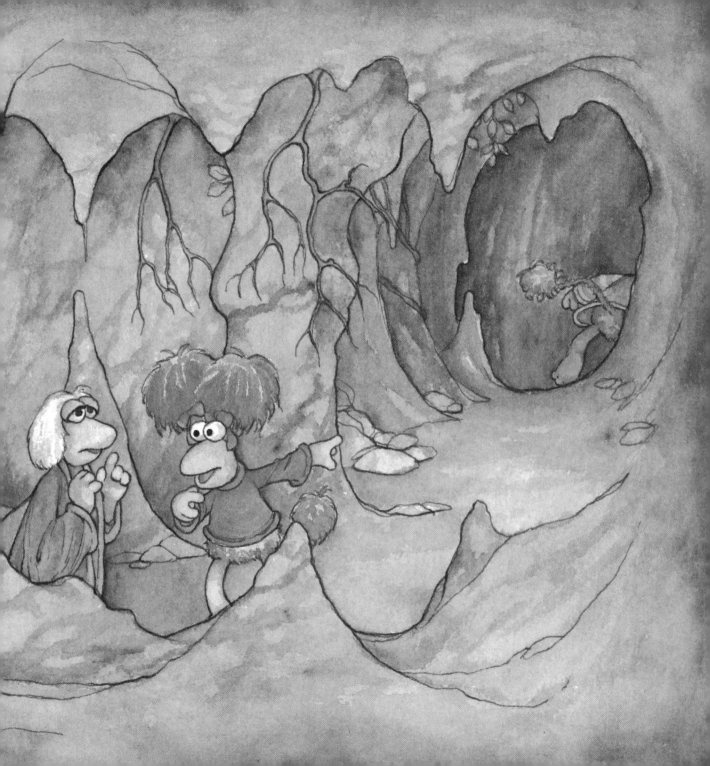

We followed through a tunnel.
We turned when he turned right.

We followed close behind him,
Just staying out of sight,

Until the tunnel got so dark,
It seemed a lot like night.

The dark got even darker,
Darker still, like deepest sleep.
The dark was very quiet
And no Fraggle made a peep.

And somewhere near I thought I heard
Some cavern crawlies creep.

Boober cried, "We're lost! We're lost!
We've traveled round and round!"

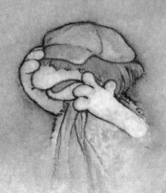

"We must keep calm," said Mokey,
"For we surely will be found."

Then Red said, "Wait a minute!
I think I hear a sound!"

We waited there forever
(At least it seemed that long!),
And then across the darkness,
Gobo's voice came, clear and strong.
"I bet you think you're lost," he said.
"But, luckily, you're wrong.

"Stay close to me and we will be
Five Fraggles—homeward bound!"

Then Gobo led us left and right.
He led us all around.
At last the caves got bright
And we were on familiar ground.

"We never should have followed you.
We had no right," I said.

Mokey nodded once or twice,
And Boober hung his head.
"But tell us, please—we're on our knees.
Where do you go?" asked Red.

"A quiet cave?" guessed Mokey,
"Where a secret river flows?"

"A cavern," Boober wondered,
"Where the speckled mushroom grows?"

"I go there when I want to think
What makes a radish grow.
Or when I want to count how many
Things there are to know.
Or when the world's too fast for me
And I want someplace slow.

"But this exact location
Will have to stay unknown.
Like everyone, I need a place
Where I can be alone.

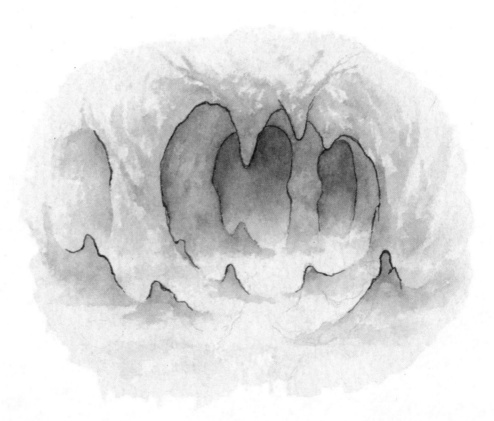

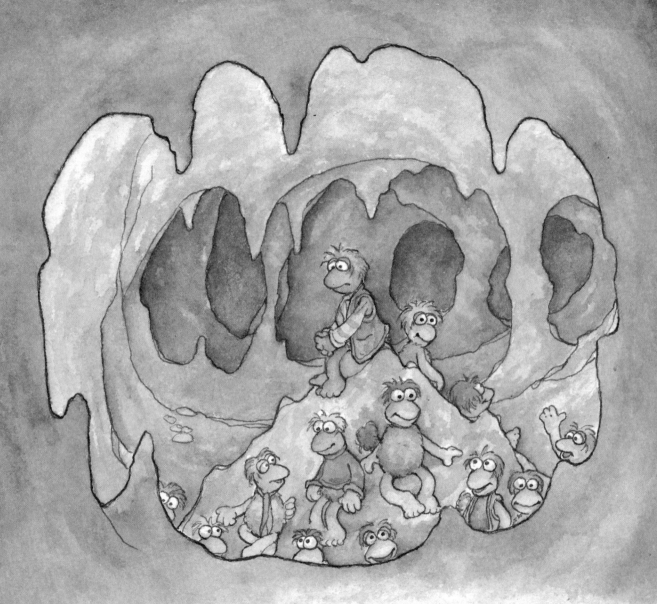

And if I told where my place was,
It wouldn't be my own."

Now, do we know where Gobo goes?
What did we really find?
I guess we know—we sort of got
An answer of a kind.

We do, but then we don't.
(I never can make up my mind.)

So no one knows where Gobo goes,
You'll still hear Fraggles say.

No one knows where Gobo goes
When Gobo goes away.

Yes, no one knows, and I suppose
That's how it's bound to stay.